JACK RUSSELL:
Dog Detective

JACK RUSSELL: Dog Detective

The Buried Biscuits

DARREL & SALLY ODGERS

SCHOLASTIC INC.

New York   Toronto   London   Auckland   Sydney
Mexico City   New Delhi   Hong Kong   Buenos Aires

ISBN-13: 978-0-545-03336-7
ISBN-10: 0-545-03336-5

First published by Scholastic Press in 2007.
Text copyright © 2007 by Sally and Darrel Odgers.
Cover design copyright © 2006 by Lake Shore Graphics.
Dog, Frisbee, courtesy of the Cansick family.
Interior illustrations by Janine Dawson.
Interior illustrations copyright © 2007 Scholastic Australia.

12 11 10 9 8 7 6 5 4 3 2 1   7 8 9 10 11 12/0

Printed in the U.S.A.
First Scholastic printing, December 2007

Dear Readers,

The story you've just started is about me and my friends, and how we solved the Case of the Buried Biscuits. To save time, I'll introduce all of us to you now. Of course, if you know us already, you can trot off to Chapter One.

I am Jack Russell, Dog Detective. I live with my landlord, Sarge, in Doggeroo. Sarge detects human-type crimes. I have the important job of detecting crimes that deal with dogs. I'm a Jack Russell terrier, so I am dogged and intelligent.

Next door to Sarge and me live Auntie Tidge and Foxy. Auntie Tidge is wonderful. She has dog biscuits. Foxy is not so wonderful. He's a fox terrier (more or less). He used to be a street dog and a thief, but he's reformed now. Auntie Tidge has even gotten rid of his fleas. Foxy sometimes helps me with my cases.

Uptown Lord Setter (Lord Red for short) lives in Uptown House with Caterina Smith. Lord Red means well, but he isn't very bright.

We have other friends in Doggeroo, too. These include Polly the dachshund, Jill Russell, the squekes, Ralf Boxer, and Shuffle the pug. Then there's Fat Molly Cat from the library.

That's all you need to know, so let's start Chapter One.

Yours doggedly,

Jack Russell—the detective with a nose for crime

Fog Fight

The Case of the Buried Biscuits began early one morning. First, there was the fight with Foxy. Then, there were the boys, and the burrows at the nature preserve. But I'd better start at the beginning.

There was a thick white fog that morning. I climbed out of my basket and *sniff-sniffed* down the steps. I trotted across the lawn and did what dogs do. Then I made a quick **nose map**.

Jack's Map

1. My dinner bowl.

2. The bone Auntie Tidge gave me on
   Thursday.

3. Boys with sticks.

4. *Rabbits in the nature preserve.*

5. *Fat Molly Cat, stalking a bird.*

6. ***Unspecial biscuits.***

It was time to plan my day. The
bone was picked clean, but the boys
had sticks to throw. Sticks need a dog
to catch them. Or I could hunt rabbits
at the nature preserve with Polly Smote.
Pawhaps I might **terrier-ize** Fat
Molly.

On the other paw, Foxy and I had
done that on Friday.

I might visit Jill Russell down at
the station. I hadn't seen her for a
while. Or how about a **Jack-snack**? I

sniff-sniffed again. Dog biscuits. Auntie Tidge gives me **special biscuits**, but these smelled like the unspecial kind. I smelled icing and jam. Maybe Sarge had put one out for me as a surprise? I checked my bowl. No biscuits. Maybe Foxy had some? I decided to pay my best pal a visit.

I got into Foxy's yard (never mind how). I checked his bowl, but it was empty.

The boys passed by on the other side of the fence. A bird twittered. Foxy snored. If there *were* biscuits around he hadn't noticed. I began to **pawtrol** the **pawrimeter**.

Again I smelled biscuits. I **Jack-yapped** to explain I wanted some. The boys took off running, and I heard a soft thud as something landed in Auntie Tidge's herb garden.

I was sniffing for clues when something bit the back of my neck.

"Gotcha!" snarled a voice.

Jacks are nimble, Jacks are quick. Jacks are always ready for a fight. I tugged free and snapped my **Jack-jaws** around a hairy leg. Someone yelped. Sharp teeth closed on my tail. I yelped. Teeth clashed, ears flapped. Foxy and I wrestled through the herb garden, squashing the garlic. I snarled.

"Jack! Cut that out! *Jack*!"

Sarge was calling, but a Jack on a mission never gets distracted. My mission was winning this fight.

"*Jack!*" Sarge sounded angry.

"Foxy Woxy! Is someone hurting you?" That was Auntie Tidge.

Splooooosh! A bucket of cold water landed on my back.

I spluttered. So did my **oppawnent**. He snarled. "I'll get you for this, Jack Russell!"

I snarled back. "You and whose army, Foxy?"

"Me, my teeth, and I!" My oppawnent nastily nipped my nose.

I yelped, and **Jack-jumped** onto his back, snapping my fangs.

"Jack! Leave Foxy alone!" Sarge loomed out of the fog and grabbed my collar. Then he picked me up and carried me back to my yard.

Jack's Facts

If a Jack is attacked, humans come to the rescue.
They always turn up when the Jack has gotten the upper paw.
Then they blame the Jack for the attack.
This is a fact.

Behind me, I heard Auntie Tidge arguing with Foxy. "No, Foxy, stop it. Put that nasty thing down. You can't have it."

Jack's Glossary

Nose map. *Way of storing information collected by the nose.*

Unspecial biscuits. *The kind of biscuits people eat.*

Paw-haps. *Perhaps.*

Terrier-ize. *Frighten.*

Jack-snack. *A snack for a Jack.*

Special biscuits. *Auntie Tidge makes these. They don't harm terrier teeth.*

Pawtrol. *Patrol, done by a dog.*

Pawrimeter. *The outside of a dog's terrier-tory.*

Jack-yap. *A loud, piercing yap made by a Jack Russell terrier.*

Jack-jaws. *The splendid set of teeth owned by a Jack Russell.*

Oppawnent. *An opponent; a dog you happen to be fighting.*

Jack-jump. *A very athletic leap done by a Jack Russell.*

# At the Shop

The fog was gone by lunchtime, but Foxy was still angry. He wouldn't tell me what Auntie Tidge had taken away from him.

"Unfair! Unfair!" he yapped from the other side of the hedge. "A dog has a right to defend his **terrier-tory!**"

"A dog has a right to visit his pal," I snarled.

"A decent dog doesn't enter without **pawmission!**" snapped Foxy.

"**Pawlite** dogs don't snore when a pal visits!" I growled.

"Foxy Woxy? Stop it!" That was

Auntie Tidge.

Sarge came out and clipped on my leash. It was time for our Saturday walk.

I leaned toward the nature preserve, but Sarge said we had to go shopping.

I leaned harder and muttered, "*Rrrrrrrrr,*" to show what I thought of shopping.

"Don't you growl at me, Jack," said Sarge.

Jack's Facts

Bad dogs growl at their people. Grrrrrr.
Good dogs sometimes mutter at their people. Rrrrrrr.
Muttering is not the same thing as growling.
This is a fact.

On the way to Tina Boxer's shop, I sniffed the air. I smelled Fat Molly and my bone, but no more biscuits.

I tried to put the morning out of my mind.

At Dora Barkins's house, the three squekes yipped in their yard, doing what squekes do.

"We went to the preserve," they yipped. "We saw rabbits. We saw boys. We chased sticks. We saw burrows. We—"

"Hurry up, Jack," interrupted Sarge. He was still cranky with me.

At the library, Fat Molly Cat was sunning herself on the steps. "*Yow-sptttt!*" she spat. I don't speak Cat, but I know swearing when I hear it.

I muttered at her, "*Rrrrrrrrrr,*" and
Molly spat again.

"Jack!" Sarge tugged my leash.

At Tina Boxer's shop, Sarge
clipped my leash to a railing. "Stay
there, Jack," he ordered. The shop bell
tinkled as he went inside. I heard Ralf
Boxer yapping behind the shop.

Jack's Facts

People say "Stay" when they tie a dog to a railing.
Dogs tied to railings have no choice but to stay.
*People are sometimes **im-paw-sible**.*
This is a fact.

The bell tinkled again. A woman came out of the shop. I *sniff-sniffed* the air and detected lamb chops and bread. She hadn't bought biscuits.

Walter Barkly came out with a bulging shopping bag. I *sniff-sniffed* the air. Walter Barkly had bought a roast chicken.

Gloria Smote tied Polly to the railing beside me. I sneezed and **snortled**.

Polly smelled of Pooch Polish.

Polly jabbed me with her sharp dachshund nose. "I went to see Jill Russell. I bet you didn't. Jill Russell has a secret."

Gloria Smote came out. She had bought more Pooch Polish.

Clack-clock-tonk. Spanggg! Clack-clock-tonk. Spanggg! Two boys were coming toward the shop. One had more freckles on his face than a Dalmatian. He was kicking a can. The other ran a stick along the fence. *Clack-clock-tonk. Clack-clock-tonk.* I pricked up my ears. These smelled like the boys who had passed my terrier-tory this morning. Was that a whiff of biscuit?

The boy, Kick, stopped kicking

and stared at me. "That's Sergeant Russell's dog. We'd better go." He and the boy, Stick, turned and scooted away.

Jack's Glossary

Terrier-tory. *A territory belonging to a terrier.*

Pawmission. *Permission, given by a dog.*

Pawlite. *Polite, for dogs.*

Im-paw-sible. *Impossible.*

Snortled. *A snuffle and a snort, caused by proximity to soap.*

Biscuit Mystery

When we got home, I checked on Foxy.

Foxy lifted his lip. He was still angry, but he was ready to talk. "Auntie Tidge is angry with me," he complained. "Auntie Tidge blamed me for the biscuits you smashed in her garden. She took the biscuits away."

"I didn't put biscuits in her herb garden. Those boys threw them over the fence this morning."

Foxy snarled. "What boys? I didn't see any boys."

"You were snoring."

"What boys would throw away biscuits?"

Foxy had a point. I trotted past him and peered at the herb garden. There wasn't much to see, except squashed herbs. The smell made my nose itch.

"The biscuits are gone," said Foxy. "I told you, Auntie Tidge took them away."

I *sniff-sniffed* anyway. Paw prints (mine), more paw prints (Foxy's), some shoe marks (Sarge's and Auntie Tidge's). There was still a faint scent of boy, mixed up with a whiff of biscuit. Was that chocolate? Then I saw a twist of shiny paper. I *sniff-sniffed* hard. Carefully, I gathered the evidence in my teeth.

"What do you have there?" Foxy
was bouncing around, trying to see it.

"Careful," I mumbled. "You'll
contaminate the scene."

"That's a chocolate wrapper,"
snapped Foxy. He tried to grab it out
of my mouth. "Auntie Tidge left it for
me to lick."

I spat out the evidence and
anchored it with my paw. "Don't be

silly, Foxy," I said. "This came from those boys, too."

"It's in my terrier-tory," growled Foxy. "That chocolate wrapper is rightfully mine."

I pawed the paper over and *sniff-sniffed* the other side. Had Stick or Kick touched this paper? If so, what did it mean? Before I could be sure, the paper had vanished. So had Foxy.

It was no use chasing Foxy and the chocolate wrapper, so I investigated the spot where it had been. I didn't learn much. The scents of chocolate and biscuit and boy were there, but the smell of herbs was stronger.

I went to visit Auntie Tidge. I did the **paw thing**, to show her I needed to investigate the biscuits.

"Hello, **Jackie Wackie**," she said. Then she picked me up and carried me home. "You stay here. Foxy is in trouble. He's been stealing again."

Auntie Tidge was wrong, but I couldn't tell her. Since I couldn't investigate the biscuits, I decided to investigate the boys.

The squekes had seen boys at the preserve. Were they the same ones? Had they thrown a bag of biscuits to the squekes? I decided to **interrier-gate** the squekes and find out.

I left my yard (never mind how) and trotted to Dora Barkins's place. The squekes were in the yard, **jaw-dueling**. I Jack-yapped. They stopped gnashing their fangs and yipped up to their gate.

"We were jaw-dueling. We were

being bad. Did you hear us? Did you—"

"Stop, in the name of the paw!" I commanded. "I'm investigating a biscuit mystery in Foxy's terrier-tory. Tell me about the boys at the preserve this morning."

"We chased sticks. We saw holes," said a squeke.

"We saw rabbits. We saw boys," said another.

"We—" began the third.

"Stop right there!" I Jack-yapped. "Tell me about the boys."

Jack's Glossary

Paw thing. *Up on hind legs, paws held together as if praying. Means happy excitement.*

Jackie Wackie. *Auntie Tidge is the only person allowed to call me that.*

Interrier-gate. *Official questioning, done by a terrier.*

Jaw-dueling. *Loud, ferocious jaw-to-jaw combat. No damage is done.*

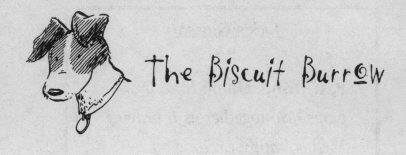

The Biscuit Burrow

The squekes had seen two boys at the preserve.

"They threw sticks," they said. "They kicked things. We chased them."

"Then what?" I asked. This *did* sound like Stick and Kick.

The squekes didn't know. "Then we saw rabbits. Then we saw a big dog digging a hole, a biscuit burrow in the bushes," they said.

Biscuits again. This sounded promising. "What kind of big dog?" I asked.

The squekes **con-furred**. "It was a
big big dog. A *hairy* big dog. A *silly*
big dog," they agreed.

I made an **inspired guess**. "Was it
Lord Red?"

"Lord Red is a big, hairy, silly
dog," agreed the squekes.

Interrier-gating three witnesses at
once was pawfully hard work.

I set off for Uptown House to
interrier-gate Red. On the way, I
decided to visit Shuffle. He lives with
Walter Barkly, who had bought a
roast chicken. If people were throwing
food around, maybe Walter Barkly
would throw the chicken.

Shuffle was lying on the porch
with his jaw on his paws. He told me
the chicken was hidden in the fridge.

Jack's Facts

People put roast chickens in the fridge.
Dogs are secretly working to learn how
to open a fridge.
One day, dogs will succeed and eat
roast chickens.
This is a fact.

While I was there, I interrier-gated
Shuffle about the biscuit burrow.

"What's a biscuit burrow?" Shuffle
wanted to know.

"The squekes said Lord Red dug a
hole at the preserve," I said. "I **sup-
paws** it must be a burrow full of
biscuits. I am on my way to interrier-
gate Red."

Shuffle got up. "I'll look for the biscuit burrow."

"Report to me when you find it," I said. "*Don't* eat the evidence."

Shuffle went into the preserve. He was moving faster than usual.

I trotted across the bridge and up the hill. Before I reached Uptown House, I heard Caterina Smith calling. "Lordie, *Lordie*! Lordieeeeee!"

<u>*Jack's Facts*</u>

People do not call a dog that is at home.
Caterina Smith was calling Red.
Therefore, Red was not at home.
This is a fact.

I **pawsed** for thought. If Red was not at home, I would visit the biscuit burrow instead. When I got to the preserve, I made a nose map.

Jack's Map

1. Shuffle the pug.

2. Chicken.

3. Lord Red.

4. A whiff of biscuit.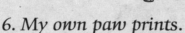

5. Boys.

6. My own paw prints.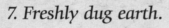

7. Freshly dug earth.

I followed my nose through the preserve until I discovered Lord Red. He was digging in some bushes. His paws were moving so fast the earth was flying backward over his tail. Shuffle was watching him.

"Stop, in the name of the paw!" I
demanded.

Red pranced up to me. "Hello,
Jack. Shuffle and I are detecting a
biscuit burrow. Come and see, Jack."

"Are you digging up the biscuits
you buried this morning?" I asked.

"I didn't bury any biscuits," said

Red. "Why would I bury biscuits? If I had biscuits, I would eat them."

"The squekes said you dug a biscuit burrow," I **pawsisted**.

"I was digging *for* a biscuit burrow," said Red. "I detected it."

"You are contaminating a crime scene," I corrected.

Red stopped prancing. His tail drooped. "Am I really, Jack? I didn't mean to do that."

I applied my **super-sniffer** to the ground. Fresh earth, Red, biscuits . . . boys.

"What do you detect, Jack?" asked Red. "Do you detect biscuits?"

"I detect boys," I said. "I know these boys. I do believe I have cracked the case!"

Jack's Glossary

Con-furred. *Talked things over, done by furry dogs.*

Inspired guess. *A clever guess made by an intelligent dog detective.*

Sup-paws. *Like suppose, but for dogs.*

Pawsed. *Stopped to think with paw upraised.*

Pawsisted. *Kept on doggedly.*

Super-sniffer. *Jack's nose in super-tracking mode.*

interrier-gation

The evidence seemed clear. I scented
boys in the fog that morning. I
whiffed them again where the biscuit
bag landed in Foxy's yard. I met them
near Tina Boxer's shop. Here was the
same scent again near the biscuit
burrow.

In some ways, boys are like dogs.
They like biscuits and sticks. They like
mud and they run around.

"Boys dug this biscuit burrow," I
announced.

"I know," said Red. He stuck his

rump in the air and sniffed hard at
the burrow.

"Then why didn't you say so?" I
asked.

Red scratched behind his ear. "I
just did. Oh, now my ear is dirty.
Caterina Smith will be mad at me."

I Jack-jumped and gave him a nip.
Red yelped. "Focus, Red," I snapped.
"Describe these boys to me."

"They had sticks. They threw
them for me. They poked them down
holes. They kicked things. They
buried biscuits. Then they saw me
watching them and ran away."

"Let's get this straight," I said. "You
saw the suspects bury biscuits in a
burrow?"

"That's right," said Red.

"In this burrow here?" I was getting to the bottom of things.

"No," said Red.

Maybe I *wasn't* getting to the bottom of things.

"One of those other burrows. Maybe it was the one Shuffle is digging up right now," said Red.

I Jack-jumped around. Shuffle was digging a new burrow. Or was he re-digging an old burrow? It was hard to be sure. Now that I looked, I saw five or six holes scattered around. By the look of Red's paws, he had dug some of them himself.

"Stop!" I commanded Shuffle.

Shuffle stopped.

I peered into the burrow. It smelled as if it used to belong to rabbits. Red and Shuffle peered in, too. At the bottom of the burrow, I detected some shiny paper. I *sniff-sniffed* hard. Now I detected biscuits inside the paper. They were unspecial biscuits with jam and strawberry icing.

"Right," I said. "There has been so much digging already, we might as well finish it. Red, get over here."

Shuffle, Red, and I began to dig. In less time than it takes Foxy to eat a sausage, we had dug up the evidence. It was a big bag of biscuits.

Carefully, I dragged it out of the burrow.

"The boys left these biscuits for us to detect," barked Red. "This is a good game." He pounced on the bag. His fangs went through the shiny paper, and a stronger smell of biscuit filled the air. I detected coconut.

A good detective asks questions about means, motive, and opportunity.

I knew the means. Stick and Kick had buried biscuits in a biscuit burrow.

The motive was obvious. Boys are like dogs. They like to dig. They like to eat. Pawhaps they save food for later. They don't want anyone else to find the food. Or maybe Red was right? Maybe they had left the biscuits for us to find? After all, they had thrown those biscuits in Foxy's terrier-tory.

The opportunity was easy. Stick and Kick had been at the preserve this morning. It must have been before I saw them at Tina Boxer's shop.

I knew all of this. What I didn't know was whether a crime had been committed.

It is not a crime to bury things, unless you do it in Auntie Tidge's vegetable patch. It's not a crime to feed dogs, unless you feed them **doggled** biscuits and **dognap** or **collar** them. So why had Stick and Kick run away when they saw me at the shop? Were they afraid I might detect their biscuits? Why hadn't they run to the preserve to guard their burrow? Did they *hope* I would detect their biscuits? Why hadn't they run to the preserve to watch me do it?

<u>Jack's Glossary</u>

Doggled. *Like disabling or drugging a racehorse by doing something that will stop it from winning a race, but done to a dog.*

Dognap. *The same as kidnap, only concerns a dog instead of a kid.*

Collar. *Grabbed by the collar during a theft or a dognapping.*

 **Identity Check**

At this stage of my deductions, I heard the sound of paper ripping.

Red had the evidence between his paws. He was peeling off the paper.

"Red!" I snapped. "What are you doing?"

"He's going to eat the biscuits," said Shuffle. He stuck his nose between Red's paws. "I want some, too." He grabbed the other end of the bag and pulled. The paper ripped and biscuits slithered out.

Red snapped up seven biscuits
and gulped them down. Shuffle
dragged the bag away, and Red
pounced on him. Shuffle bit Red's lip
and Red howled.

"Stop!" I Jack-yapped.

They paid no attention. Red trod
on Shuffle's nose, and Shuffle sneezed
and growled. Red snapped up more
biscuits and swallowed them whole.

I Jack-yapped again, then yelped as somebody bit my tail. "Gotcha!" snarled Foxy.

I Jack-jumped around. "What are you doing here?"

"I tracked you down," said Foxy. "And what do I find? You have biscuits! You said you didn't have any biscuits. You lied."

"I didn't have any then," I objected. "And I don't have them now. Red and Shuffle have them."

"Not for much longer," said Foxy. He darted under Red's belly and grabbed the biscuit bag. It was half empty and scraps of it were scattered all around the burrow.

Foxy ran off through the bushes, shedding bits of paper and biscuit.

Red and Shuffle went on growling and snuffling and rolling about.

I sidestepped them and *sniff-sniffed* around the burrow.

Right at the bottom was a corner of the paper bag. I scrabbled at it with my paws until I could lift it out. It smelled strongly of licorice. I chewed through the bag and subjected the contents to **jaw-rensic testing**.

Next, I checked the burrow Red had been digging. At the bottom, I found a box that smelled of toffee, and another bag of biscuits. I pulled them out and performed an **identity check**.

The first biscuit passed muster, so I tested another to be sure.

Jack's Facts

One biscuit may look as good as another.
One biscuit may smell as good as another.
To tell if one biscuit is as good as another, it is necessary to eat both.
This is a fact.

I was still performing identity checks when I heard a familiar voice. "Lordie, *Lordie*! Lordieeeeee!"

"Caterina Smith is calling," said Lord Red. He stopped scuffling with Shuffle and took off through the bushes.

I identity checked another biscuit.

Shuffle snorted and wheezed as he jaw-rensic tested the licorice.

We were still busy when I heard Walter Barkly calling Shuffle. Next, I heard Sarge call me.

Time to go. I scooted through the bushes, Jack-jumped into Sarge's arms, and **greeted** him. Sarge frowned at me.

"What have you been up to, Jack? Why's your tongue black?"

Jack's Facts

Chow chows' tongues are black.
Other dogs' tongues are pink.
Jack Russells' tongues are black if they've eaten licorice.
This is a fact.

I licked Sarge's face again and left a smear.

Sarge sniffed. "Smells like licorice. Where did you get that?"

Jack's Facts

A Jack Russell's nose is far **su-paw-rior** *to a human's.*
Even a human can detect the smell of licorice.
That is a fact.

I was about to show Sarge the evidence when I remembered something. Sarge didn't know about the boys. He might take the mystery biscuits away. Thinking quickly, I **Jack-knifed** out of his arms and set off for home. I was confident that he'd follow.

Jack's Glossary

Jaw-rensic testing. *Testing done by chewing evidence.*

Identity check. *Usually performed by sniffing or biting.*

Greet. *This is done by rising to the hind legs and clutching a person with the paws while slurping them up the face.*

Su-paw-rior. *Superior, the way Jack Russells are.*

Jack-knife. *A kind of sudden leap and twist performed by Jacks when they want to get down in a hurry.*

Under Arrest

Three hours later, we were all under arrest.

It was Foxy, Red, and Shuffle's fault. Some dogs don't know when to cut their losses. Other dogs just can't hold their biscuits.

Sarge caught Foxy with the end of the biscuit bag. I saw it happen. Sarge tried to get the bag. Foxy snapped at Sarge, and Sarge chased him home.

Walter Barkly caught Shuffle halfway through a licorice stick. I saw that happen, too. Shuffle growled and pulled the licorice stick until it snapped.

The biscuits Red ate disagreed with him. He made a horrible mess on Caterina Smith's carpet. I didn't see that happen, but I heard about it. Caterina Smith called Sarge and Auntie Tidge. She said she was taking Red to the vet, in case he'd been poisoned.

When Auntie Tidge heard that, she took Foxy and me to the vet. We all met up in the waiting room.

"Hello," Red said when he spotted Foxy and me. He didn't jump around. His nose looked dry. "I'm sick from a poisoned biscuit. What if I die?"

"We're not speaking to you," growled Foxy.

"I'm really sick," said Red. "My tummy hurts. My head hurts. My teeth hurt. My lip hurts. My ear hurts. Those biscuits were poisoned."

"**Dogwash**!" I said.

"Why do I hurt, then?"

"You had a fight with Shuffle," I reminded him. "He bit your lip. And I bit your ear, to make you pay attention."

"You didn't bite my belly," moaned Red. "The poisoned biscuits bit my belly."

"You ate too much," I said. "Foxy and Shuffle ate the same biscuits. So did I. We're not sick."

Just then, it was our turn to see the vet. We didn't enjoy it.

The vet poked Foxy and me. He looked in our ears and eyes. He stuck things under our tails. He said we looked fine but that we should be kept under observation.

"Dogs that wander around can eat all sorts of bad things," he said.

Auntie Tidge took us home. She called Dora Barkins and Gloria Smote and told them what the vet had said. After that, half the dogs in Doggeroo were under arrest.

"It's for your own good, Jackie Wackie," said Auntie Tidge as she shut me and Foxy in the shed. "You've both been naughty boys. Imagine stealing biscuits! This time you were lucky, but next time it might be a different story."

I didn't feel lucky. It was boring in the shed. I chewed my **squeaker-bone** for a while. After that there was nothing to do except listen to Foxy complain.

I decided to work on the case, although I still wasn't sure that there was a case.

"Why would the biscuit boys run away from me?" I asked Foxy.

"They saw your ugly mug," snapped Foxy.

"Dogwash," I said. "They knew who I was. They didn't say 'that's a dog,' they said 'that's Sergeant Russell's dog.'"

"Maybe they ran away from someone else," said Foxy. "Were there any **bulldogs** around? Bulldogs use terrier toothpicks. They probably eat boys for breakfast."

"They ran away from *me*," I pawsisted. Then I remembered something. "They ran away from me *twice*."

"Once would be enough for most boys," muttered Foxy. He scratched his ribs.

"The first time was when I first

detected the biscuits," I explained. "I was pawtrolling—er—" I stopped because I remembered where I had been at the time.

"Don't mind me," growled Foxy. "You were pawtrolling the pawrimeter of *my* terrier-tory."

"Only because you were asleep," I said. "Otherwise you'd have been pawtrolling yourself." Foxy muttered at me then, but I pretended not to hear. "I detected biscuits and Jack-yapped to tell the boys I wanted some. They threw the bag over the fence and ran away."

Foxy's eyes gleamed. "They thought you were me," he said. "Since you were in my terrier-tory and it was foggy. Therefore, they were running away from *me*. It makes sense. It's a well-known fact that fox terriers are more feared than Jack Russells."

Jack's Facts

Jack Russells have facts.
Other dogs think they have facts.
What they really have are opinions.
Jack Russells' facts really are facts.
This is a fact.

"They knew who I was at the shop," I reminded him.

Foxy wasn't listening. He was still **chasing his line of reasoning**. "It was really me they were running away from. Therefore, they thought I was the one who wanted the biscuits," he said. "That means they threw the bag of biscuits into my terrier-tory for me. And *that* means Auntie Tidge had no right to take them."

I knew there was a flaw in Foxy's reasoning somewhere.

Jack's Glossary

Dogwash. *Nonsense.*

Squeaker-bone. *Item for exercising teeth. Not to be confused with a toy.*

Bulldog. *Large dog with more muscles than brains.*

Chasing his line of reasoning. *Dogs like to chase things.*

Jill Russell's Surprise

That night, Sarge made me sleep in
the kitchen. Next morning, he let me
out to do what dogs do. Then he
called me in again.

After a few minutes, I headed for
the **dog door**. It was jammed shut. I
prodded it with my nose a few times.
I scratched with my paw. I whined
loudly.

"Stop that, Jack," said Sarge.

I did the paw thing to show him I
had important detective business
outside.

"You just came in," said Sarge. "I'll take you out for a walk tomorrow. I have to see the Johnsons about some trouble at the newsstand."

I pricked up my ears. The Johnsons are Jill Russell's people. Jill Russell is **ace**. I did the paw thing again.

"Tomorrow," said Sarge.

Jacks are good at escaping from yards. Jacks jump over. Jacks burrow under. Jacks crawl through.

Jacks are not so good at escaping from houses. Houses have roofs. Houses have wooden floors. Houses have walls. Windows can be locked. Dog doors can be jammed. That's why I was still in the house the next day.

Sarge put on my leash after breakfast. Foxy was standing on a chair in Auntie Tidge's kitchen. I saw him banging on the window with his paws.

"Unfair! Unfair!" he yapped. "If Jack can go out, I can go out!"

He was still yapping as we walked along the street.

At the station, Jack Johnson bent down to rub my ears. "Jill has a surprise for you, Jack." He grinned at Sarge.

"What's the problem with the newsstand?" asked Sarge.

While Sarge and Jack Johnson talked, I made a nose map.

Jack's Map

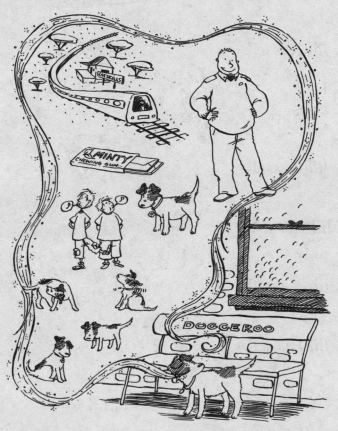

1. Trains.

2. Jack Johnson.

3. Chewing gum.

4. Jill Russell.

5. Boys.

6. Jill Russell.

7. Jill Russell.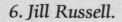

8. Jill Russell.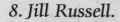

9. Jill Russell.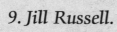

What? I shook my head and
sneefled to clear my nose. There was
always plenty to smell at the station,
but why was I smelling Jill Russell
more than once? I *sniff-sniffed* again.

Don't tell me my super-sniffer wasn't working? *Sniff-sniff.*

I couldn't make it out, so I concentrated on another scent. Boys. Sarge and Jack Johnson were heading for the newsstand, so I went, too. I had my nose to the ground, because I knew that scent. It was Kick and Stick, the mysterious biscuit boys. I looked around, but couldn't see them.

"It's vandals," said Jack Johnson. "I could understand if they were hungry, but they just break them up and throw them around."

"Just biscuits?" asked Sarge.

"Toffee, chocolate, licorice, biscuits . . . all kinds of things," said Jack Johnson. "Just a few bags here and there, but it's annoying."

"Scattered around, you say?"

"Yes. There's no point to it."

"That might explain what the dogs have been eating," said Sarge. "Have you seen any strangers hanging around?"

Jack Johnson laughed. "Of course. It's a station."

Sarge laughed, too. "I can't do much without any leads," he said. "If you see anyone hanging around, give me a call."

Jack Johnson glanced at the clock. "There are no trains due for a while, so let's bring Jack to see Jill's surprise."

Sarge and I followed him to the house next door to the station. I smelled Jill Russell again and whined a greeting.

"In here," said Jack Johnson. He opened a door. Sarge and I went in.

Jill Russell was lying in her basket. When she saw us, she got out and poked me with her nose. Then she went back to the basket. I followed her and looked down at a litter of pups. They smelled like Jill Russell, but they were hardly bigger than rats. They squeaked like rats, too.

"What do you think of the puppies, Jack?" asked Jack Johnson.

I *sniff-sniffed* carefully. Jill Russell looked at me out of the corner of her eye and muttered. "Watch it, Jack," she said. "Keep your nose to yourself."

Sarge bent down and peered into the basket. "Nice little fellows, aren't they?" he said. "What do you think, Jack?"

I *sniff-sniffed* again and wagged my tail. One of the pups squirmed over and tried to bite my nose. I felt my tail wagging harder.

Jack's Facts

Dogs wag tails.
Now and then, tails wag dogs.
This happens if a dog is especially pleased.
This is a fact.

Sarge laughed. "It seems that Jack approves of his puppies," he said. "Well . . . thanks for showing us. See you later."

> ### Jack's Glossary
>
> **Dog door.** *A door especially for dogs.*
>
> **Ace.** *Great, fine, the very best.*
>
> **Sneefle.** *A snorting sneeze, done to clear the nose.*

A Bit Tied Up

It was ace to see the puppies, but I
had to escape from Sarge to work on
my case.

Foxy was under arrest. So were
Polly, Shuffle, and the squekes. So was
Red. Jill Russell was free, but she
wouldn't leave the puppies.

What to do? What to do?

That's when Sarge got a call on
his radio. He frowned. "There's some
kind of trouble at Tina Boxer's shop.
I have to run. Could I leave Jack

with you?"

"Of course," said Jack Johnson. He reached out for my leash.

"Thanks!" said Sarge. "I'll be back as soon as I can." He hurried off. I pulled toward Jill Russell and whined. Then I did the paw thing.

"You're an old softy, Jack," said Jack Johnson. "Have another look, then I'll tie you up. I don't want you chasing Sarge."

Being tied up was not part of my plan. Neither was chasing Sarge. When Jack Johnson had gone, I leaned toward the basket.

"Get your nose away from my babies," snapped Jill Russell. She curled around the puppies.

I whined, in case Jack Johnson was
listening. Then I interrier-gated Jill
Russell.

"Have you seen two boys near the
newsstand?"

"Don't be silly, Jack," said Jill
Russell. "I have puppies. Who cares
about boys?"

"These boys smell of unspecial
biscuits," I said doggedly.

Jill Russell snorted. "Most boys do."

"They kick things and rattle sticks," I said.

"*Them*." Jill Russell muttered. "*Rrrrrrr*."

"You saw them?"

"I *heard* them first," snapped Jill Russell. "They frightened the pups. They made poor little Preacher cry." She nudged a boy pup with her nose.

"When was this?" I pawsisted.

"Yesterday," said Jill Russell. "They came kicking and rattling around while Jack Johnson was taking care of a train. They were near the newsstand, but I chased them away." She muttered again. "They dropped some licorice."

"You are a **star witness**, Jill Russell," I said. "I should have come to you in the first place."

Jill Russell rolled the boy puppy on his back and started licking his tummy.

"Those boys are Stick and Kick," I said. "I believe they stole that licorice from the newsstand. I suspect they also stole biscuits and buried them in a burrow."

Jill Russell stared at me over the puppies. "You're crazy, Jack. People don't steal biscuits. They buy them in the shop."

"Not always, Jill Russell," I said. "Sometimes they steal them. We detectives understand these things. I must catch them in the act and deliver them to Sarge."

"Why?" asked Jill Russell. "Why should you care if boys steal unspecial biscuits, Jack? They're not special biscuits."

That gave me paws for thought. Maybe Jill was right. Why *should* I care?

"Stealing things is bad," I said. "When boys steal biscuits and bury them, bad things happen to dogs that dig them up." I told her about Red and our visit to the vet. Then I told her how we were all under arrest.

"That's easy," she said. "Just don't dig for biscuits."

"I won't," I said, "but how am I going to stop Foxy? You know what he's like around food. And Red won't stop. As soon as he forgets his bellyache, he'll be digging again. So will Shuffle."

Jill Russell said it had nothing to do with her.

"What about your puppies, then?" I said. "Do you want *them* to dig up unspecial biscuits and get bellyaches?"

Jill Russell muttered. She had obviously changed her mind. "You'd better go, Jack. The quicker you solve this, the better."

"I'm a bit tied up at the moment," I pointed out.

Jill Russell climbed out of the basket and came over to me. She inspected me from head to tail. Then she put her paw on my head and pushed me down, as if I were a puppy. "You'll have to pull out of your collar," she said. "That leash is too tough to bite through."

"I can't," I said. "It's too tight. And you know what happens to dogs that lose their collars."

"They get put in the pound," said Jill Russell. "Chin up, ears down, and *pullll!*"

Jack's Glossary

Star witness. *A witness who has good sense.*

Pawformance

I did what Jill Russell said, and *pulllled.* I pulled until I thought my ears would come off. I felt my collar slide up and up, then I Jack-knifed. One of my ears popped free.

The collar slid over my nose and landed on the ground. It lay there looking empty. My neck felt funny without it.

"Hurry!" snapped Jill Russell.

I shook myself hard, then raced out the door. Some dogs might have tracked Sarge to Tina Boxer's shop.

Instead, I scooted back toward the
nature preserve. I didn't go in, but
fixed myself a **steak-out** on the edge.
I made a thorough nose map.

Jack's Map

1. *Shuffle the pug.*

2. *Licorice.*

3. *Lord Red.*

4. *A whiff of biscuit, getting stronger all the time.*

5. *Boys.*

I sneefled and sniffed again. Yes, boys. Stick and Kick were heading for the preserve.

Boys are like dogs. They have favorite places to hide things they don't want found. They must have stolen some biscuits from Tina Boxer's shop.

Now I saw it all. They hadn't been hiding biscuits for dogs. They had hidden them for themselves. The bag they threw in Foxy's yard must have been meant as a **Jack-straction**. When I Jack-yapped, they had thrown the biscuits to keep me from following them.

My steak-out soon paid off. Kick and Stick passed by me, heading for the burrows in the bushes. Their jackets were bulging with what my super-sniffer said were unspecial biscuits and chocolate bars.

"We might need a new hiding place," said Stick.

"Nah." Kick kicked a can. "Those dogs are all away now. We can camp out Friday night."

What could I do now? Some dog detectives might **pawform** an arrest, but Jack Russells aren't the biggest dogs in the world. I let the biscuit boys go past. Then I went back to the station for backup and set up a **pawformance** for Jack Johnson.

I Jack-yapped over and over. I growled and howled. I ran and yipped. Jack Johnson rushed out of the station.

"Jack! How did you get loose? I told Sarge I'd look after you!"

I darted up to Jack Johnson and greeted him. Then I Jack-knifed out of his arms and darted away again. Jack Johnson followed me. I almost let him catch me, but I kept on jumping. I trotted off toward the preserve.

Jack Johnson came running after me. "Jack, Jack, come back!"

I tore past my steak-out and dived into the bushes, with Jack Johnson chasing after me. That's how he caught Stick and Kick red-handed, burying biscuits in the burrows.

Jack Johnson stopped trying to grab me. He grabbed Stick and Kick instead. Then he made them go back to the station. He **terrier-phoned** Sarge at Tina Boxer's shop, and Sarge came to take the biscuit boys into custody.

A couple of days later, Foxy said he saw them scrubbing the station newsstand. Ralf Boxer said they planted flowers around Tina Boxer's shop. Red said he saw them walking the squekes. They were so busy they didn't have time to steal any biscuits.

I didn't see any of that. I was too busy helping Jill Russell with the puppies. My pawformance had frightened them a little. Not much, because Jack Russell puppies are the bravest pups around. "You're ace," I told little Preacher, and he bit my nose.

Jack's Glossary

Steak-out. *Hiding and watching for pupetrators.*

Jack-straction. *Distracted by a Jack, or an attempt to distract a Jack.*

Pawform. *Do, for dogs.*

Pawformance. *A splendid act put on by a talented dog.*

Terrier-phone. *Something that rings.*

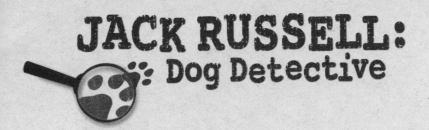

JACK RUSSELL: Dog Detective

Catch up with your favorite dog detective in all of Jack's other adventures:

COMING SOON!

JACK RUSSELL: DOG DETECTIVE #8
THE KITNAPPED CREATURE

I had smelled that cat and heard that cat-erwaul before. I raced as fast as Preacher could go. My mind raced faster. I added one to one and one and came up with one.

Jack's Facts

*If you take one horrible familiar cat-erwaul
And add one familiar smell and one yelling human
You get one familiar monster cat.
This is a fact.*